I Like the Way You Are

I Like the Way You Are

by **Eve Bunting**

illustrated by **John O'Brien**

Clarion Books • New York

Clarion Books
a Houghton Mifflin Company imprint
215 Park Avenue South, New York, NY 10003
Text copyright © 2000 by Edward D. Bunting and Anne E. Bunting Family Trust
Illustrations copyright © 2000 by John O'Brien

The illustrations were executed in watercolor and pen and ink.
The text was set in 17–point Adobe Caslon.

Printed in Singapore.

Library of Congress Cataloging-in-Publication Data

Bunting, Eve.
I like the way you are / by Eve Bunting ; illustrated by John O'Brien.
p.   cm.
Summary: When two turtles go to the gym, plant a garden, see a movie, eat out,
and go on a night hike, they discover that you do not have to like
the same things in order to be friends.
ISBN 0-395-89066-7
[1. Turtles Fiction. 2. Friendship Fiction.] I. O'Brien, John, 1953– ill. II. Title.
PZ7.B91527Iaat   2000
[Fic]—dc21   99–16607
CIP

TWP   10   9   8   7   6

To Tory and Erin,
I like the way you are.
—E.B.

For Tess
—J.O'B.

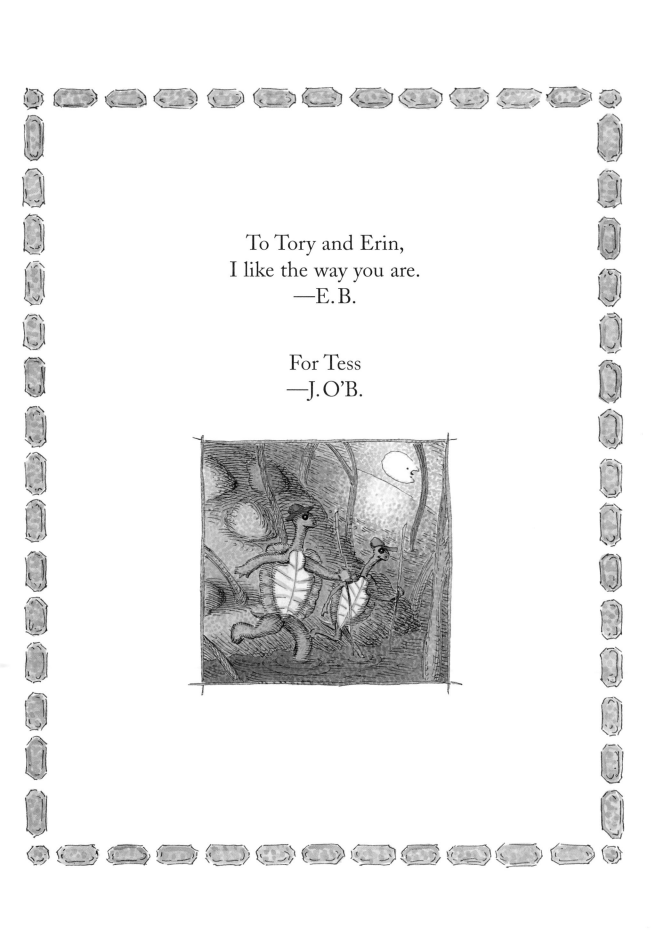

Contents

At the Gym

 urtle and his friend Spotted Turtle went to
the turtle gym.

They did pull-ups and push-ups, knee bends and splits.

Turtle was very good.

His friend Spottie was not. But Turtle didn't say so.

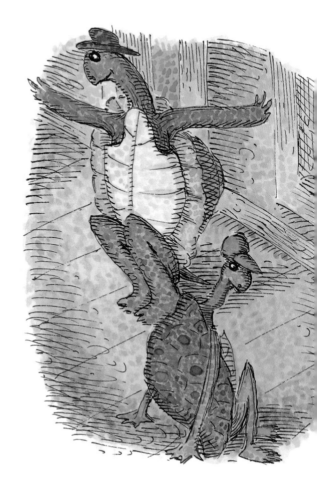

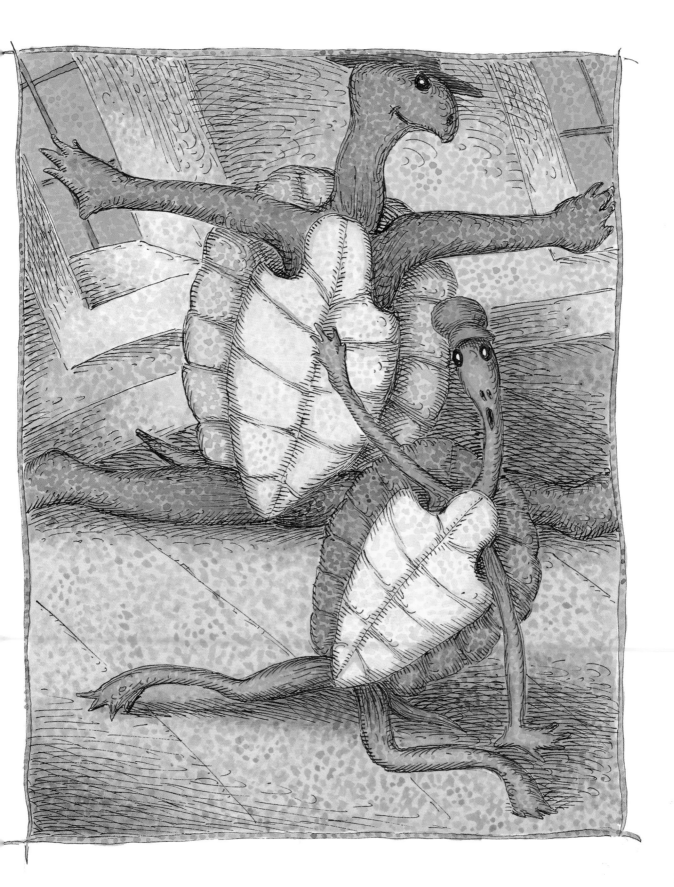

They did back rolls and helped each other get right side up
again.

Turtle was very good.

Spottie was not. But Turtle didn't say so. He didn't want to
hurt his friend's feelings.

On the way home, Spottie was gloomy. "I wasn't very good in the gym," he said.

"Don't worry," Turtle said. He thought singing might help cheer Spottie up.

"Let's sing," Turtle said. He started them off. His voice was like a barking bulldog's. *"Where the floating lily pads dance beneath the moon."*

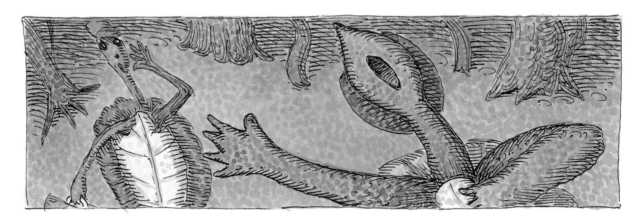

Spottie joined in. He had a beautiful voice, smooth and sweet as beetle juice.

"Oh, my!" Turtle said. "You have a beautiful voice, smooth and sweet as beetle juice."

"Thank you," Spottie said. He thought Turtle's voice was like a barking bulldog's. But he didn't say so. He didn't want to hurt his friend's feelings.

"Isn't it nice?" Turtle said. "One turtle is good at one thing. Another turtle is good at something else."

His friend agreed. "Together we are good at twice as many things."

They sang together all the way home. *"Where the floating lily pads dance beneath the moon."*

Then Turtle said, "Good night, Spottie."
And Spottie said, "Good night, Turtle."

PLOP!

PLOP!

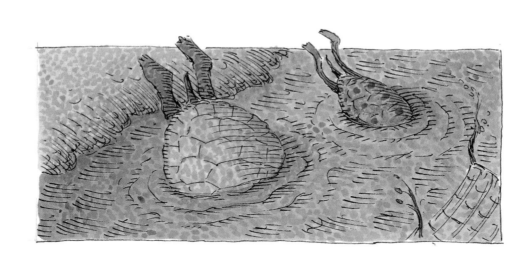

Planting a Garden

Turtle and Spottie dug up the dirt around their pond.

They got seeds.

They planted lettuce, carrots, and tomatoes.

They watered their seeds with pond water, and weeded, and watched, and waited.

Spottie sang to the new plants.
   "Be big and strong as you can be.
   Be big for Turtle and for me."
The lettuce and carrots and tomatoes grew.

Turtle sang, too, to keep the rabbits and gophers away.
   "Garrumph! Garrumph! Garrumph!"
His voice was so horrible it could scare away bears.

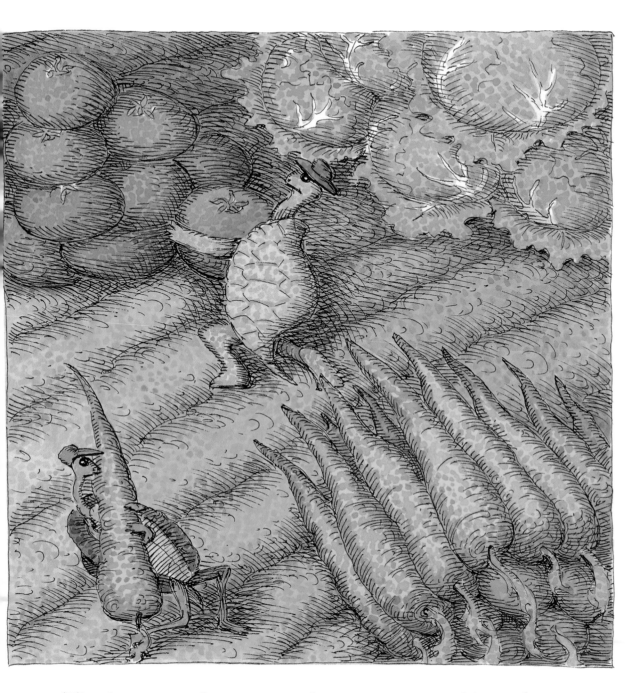

The lettuce and carrots and tomatoes grew big and strong.
"A change of menu will be good," Spottie said.
Turtle agreed. "A turtle gets tired of pond food."

Turtle and Spottie found snails in the lettuce.
They found cutworms on the tomatoes.
And they found bugs in the carrots.
"Let's eat," said Turtle.
"Yum!" said Spottie.
"Yum!" said Turtle.
"Yum! Yum!" said Spottie. "There's nothing like fresh meat with a small salad on the side."

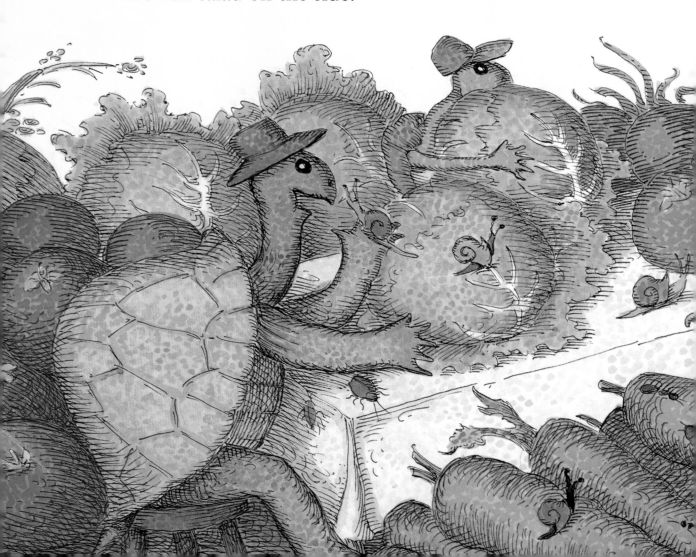

Night after night they feasted.
They brought their friends.
"Picnic! Picnic!" Turtle called.
"It's so fulfilling to grow your own food," Spottie said.
Turtle patted his stomach. "I am so full and I am so filled.
I've had enough vegetables."

Spottie nodded. "A few vegetables go a long way."
"Tonight I will not sing," Turtle said.
Because he did not sing, the rabbits and gophers came.
They carried away lettuce and carrots and tomatoes.

"It's so nice to share," Turtle said. He yawned. "Now I am a full and filled and happy turtle."

"I, too," Spottie said. "Good night, Turtle."

"Good night, my friend. Sweet dreams."

PLOP!
PLOP!

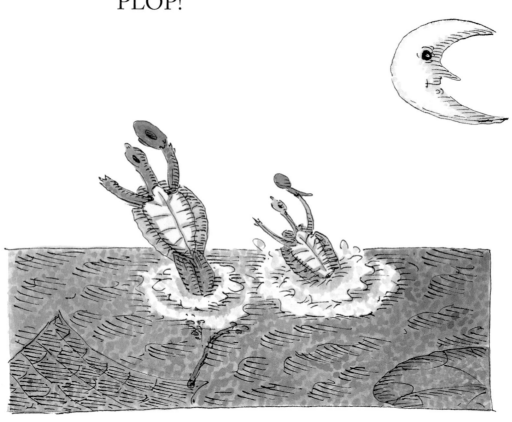

urtle and Spottie went to the movies.
The movie was called *The Frog Prince*.

"Let's share a big tub of popbugs," Turtle said. "Lots of butter, please," he told Mr. Popbug.

"I don't like butter," Spottie said.

"Then could you make it half-and-half, please, Mr. Popbug? Lots of butter on the right side of the tub, none on the left."

"Certainly," Mr. Popbug said.

"Let's share a large beetle juice," Spottie said.

"I like crab juice better," Turtle said.

"Then could you make it half-and-half, please, Mr. Juice? Crab juice on the right, beetle juice on the left. Two straws."

"Certainly," Mr. Juice said.

Turtle carried the popbugs.

Spottie carried the juice.

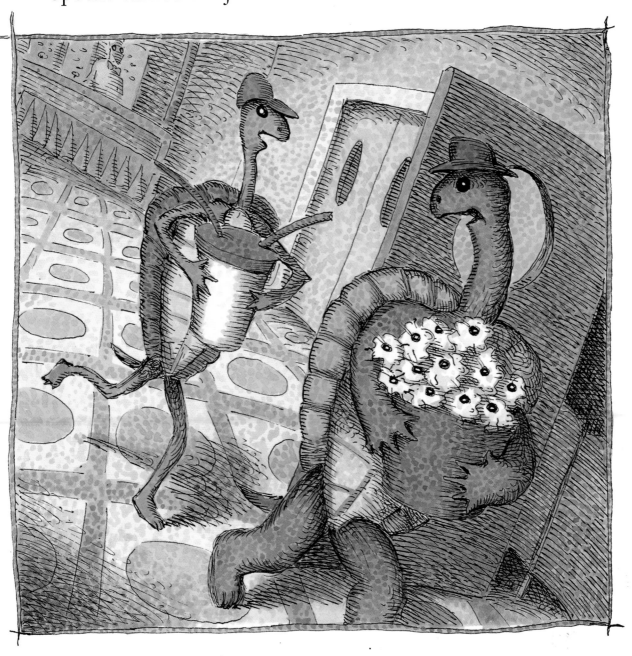

"Let's sit in the front," Turtle said.
"I like to sit in the back," Spottie told him.
"Then let's sit in the middle," said Turtle.
They sat and munched and crunched and slurped.

The movie began.

The star frog was very handsome.

But near the end, a princess kissed him. Quick as a tongue flick, he changed into an ugly prince.

Turtle and Spottie talked about it as they walked home.

"She should not have kissed that nice frog," Turtle said. "He looked like Peeper in our pond."

"It was a sad story," Spottie said. "I cried."

Turtle nodded. "I did, too. I am glad I have never met a princess. She might want to kiss me."

"If we see a princess, we will hide under our shells," Spottie said.

Turtle nodded. "Good idea."

Moonlight was shivery gold on the pond. Stars swam in the dark water.

Turtle sighed happily. "Shall we meet for breakfast?" he asked.

"I don't eat breakfast," Spottie said. "How about lunch?"

"I don't eat lunch," Turtle said. "But we could do brunch. It's halfway between breakfast and lunch," he explained.

"Sounds good," Spottie said. "Isn't it nice that we don't have to agree about everything, but we are still friends?"

"Really nice," Turtle said. "Good night, my friend."

"Good night, Turtle."

PLOP!
PLOP!

urtle took Spottie out to dine.

"You mean, to eat?" Spottie asked.

"At the Posh Place, we say dine," Turtle told him.

The Posh Place was very fancy. The waiters wore white aprons and bow ties.

Spottie looked at the menu. "I can't read the words," he said.

"They are in French," Turtle told him.

"We can't read French," Spottie said.

"Shh!" Turtle said. "Pretend. In the Posh Place you must act posh."

"What will you have?" the waiter asked.

Turtle pointed. "This and this."

"*Merci*," the waiter said.

"I think *merci* means 'thank you' in French," Turtle whispered.

"But we don't know what we're getting," Spottie said.

"Shh!" Turtle said. "Pretend we do."

They listened to the music.

They watched the dancing.

Their first dish came. It was mushy, red and yellow striped. "This is the special Posh Place salad," the waiter said. "Enjoy!"

"*Merci,*" Turtle told the waiter.

Spottie took a bite. It was awful. But he didn't say so. He didn't want to hurt Turtle's feelings

Turtle filled up his fork. He filled up his mouth. "*Blah!*" he said. "*Blah! Bloot! Barf!*"

Turtle's eyes bulged. His tongue hung out. It was striped red and yellow. "I'm going to be sick!" he yelled.

Their waiter ran over. "Out!" he said. "Nobody can be sick in the Posh Place."

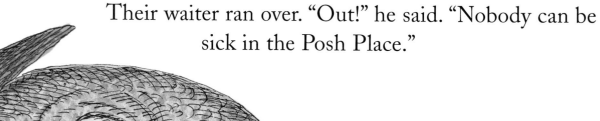

Turtle and Spottie stood on the sidewalk.

Turtle looked sad.

"How about going to McMollusks?" Spottie asked, to cheer him up.

Turtle cheered up.

They each got slug nuggets and cricket fries.

They ate as they walked.

"I'm sorry about the Posh Place," Turtle said. "Pretending doesn't work very well."

"We could learn French," Spottie said. "Then we will know not to get the red and yellow striped stuff."

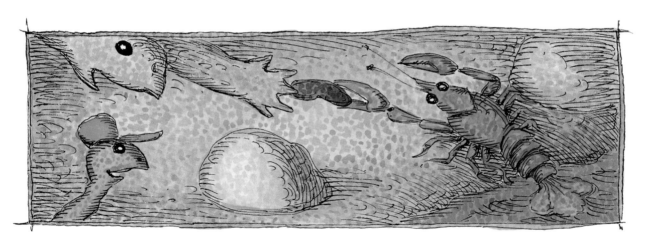

A crawfish crawled at the edge of their pond. He was lucky they were not hungry anymore. They gave him the last of their slug nuggets.

Turtle sighed. "I guess I am who I am," he said. "I am not who I am not."

"I like the way you are," Spottie told him.

"Well, *merci*," Turtle said. "I like the way you are, too."

"*Merci*," Spottie said. "Good night, Turtle."

"Good night, my friend."

PLOP!
PLOP!

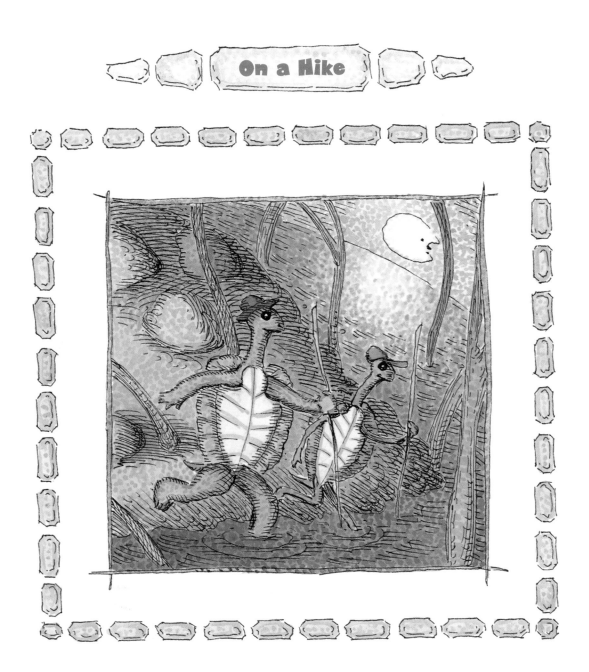

urtle and Spottie went on a night hike.
They walked up a hill and through a marsh.
"Walking makes the legs strong," Turtle said.
"It also makes the heart strong," Spottie said.

33

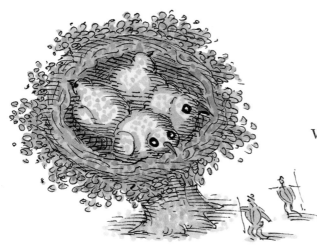

They paddled across a stream.
They walked under a wide,
wide tree where birds nested.
A coyote came by.

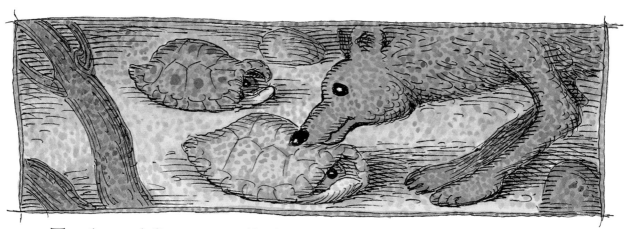

Turtle and Spottie pulled their heads and legs and tails
under their shells.

Coyote sniffed around them. He went away.

"Shells are good to hide from coyotes," Turtle said.

"And to hide from kissing princesses," Spottie said.

The moon sailed white in the sky behind them.
It had rained. Worms wriggled around their feet.
They snacked as they walked.

"When you have a friend to walk with, you go far, far,
far," Turtle said. "Slow, slow, slow. But far, far, far. Sometimes
you go too far. You forget you have to go back."

"That's true. And sometimes you forget that you are
getting tired," Spottie said.

They stopped and looked at each other.

"I think we have come far, far, far," Turtle said.

"At least far, far," Spottie said. "And I am so tired. I am so tired my shell feels heavy."

"That means you are very tired," Turtle said.

The moon sailed white in the sky in front of them.

They walked under the wide, wide tree where birds nested.

Worms wriggled around their feet.

But they were too tired even to snack.

They paddled across the stream.

"I have an idea," Turtle said. "I will carry you for a while, and that way you can rest."

"Then I will be rested, and I will carry you," Spottie said.

"That is a splendid idea," Turtle said.

Turtle carried his friend across the marsh.

Spottie carried his friend down the hill. "It is good that our legs and our hearts are strong," he said.

And there was their pond.

The lily pads slept on the cool water.

The flowers had closed themselves tight against the night.

"It is good to have a friend to walk with. And to carry you when you are tired," Turtle said.

"It would be hard to carry yourself," Spottie said. "But you don't have to when you have a friend."

They smiled at each other.

"Good night, Turtle."

"Good night, my friend," Turtle said.

PLOP!
PLOP!